BIKES

by Anne Rockwell

E. P. Dutton   •   New York

Copyright © 1987 by Anne Rockwell
Published in the United States by E.P. Dutton,
2 Park Avenue, New York, N.Y. 10016
Published simultaneously in Canada by
Fitzhenry & Whiteside Limited, Toronto
Editor: Ann Durell
Printed in Hong Kong by South China Printing Co.
First Edition   COBE   10 9 8 7 6 5 4 3 2 1

Library of Congress Cataloging in Publication Data
Rockwell, Anne F.
   Bikes.

   Summary: Describes many different types of bikes,
including the unicycle, tandem bike, racing bike,
exercise bike, and trail bike.
   1. Bicycles—Juvenile literature.
[1. Bicycles and bicycling]   I. Title.
TL410.R54   1987   629.2'272   86-19923
ISBN 0-525-44287-1

Little kids ride tricycles.

Big kids ride bicycles with horns that blow.

Parents ride bicycles with seats for babies.

A unicycle is a bike with only one wheel.

A tandem bike has two seats
so friends can ride together.

Racing bikes go very fast.

Delivery bikes in big cities carry food
from stores to homes.

An exercise bike doesn't go anywhere,
but its wheel turns fast.

A motorcycle is a big bike
with a big, noisy motor.

The rider can make it jump over things.

A moped has a little motor.

A motor scooter has two little wheels
and no pedals.

Trail bikes have knobby tires that go
on dirt and through mud puddles.

This cycle has three big, fat tires.
The farmer rides it around the farm.

We ride bikes through city parks.

We ride bikes on country roads.

We ride bikes to school.

Today is my birthday.
Today I got a bicycle with training wheels.